Puf

THE KAR
AND THE CUT-THROAT

'There doesn't seem much for a princess to do these days, especially one that can only do karate.'

Belinda can't really be more wrong when she complains to her ape-monster friend, Knacker-leevee, that she's bored. For her deadly rival, Princess Saramanda, and her thuggish band of cut-throat robbers are about to launch an attack on Belinda's father's kingdom – and they're going to make sure Belinda's out of the way when they do it!

This is the second story about the Karate Princess.

Jeremy Strong has worked as a computer programmer, a caretaker, a wages clerk and at putting the jam in doughnuts. He is now a teacher – and children's writer – and lives with his family in Kent.

Other books by Jeremy Strong
in Puffin

FATBAG: THE DEMON VACUUM CLEANER
THE KARATE PRINCESS AND THE CUT-THROAT ROBBERS
THE KARATE PRINCESS
THE KARATE PRINCESS TO THE RESCUE
LIGHTNING LUCY
MY DAD'S GOT AN ALLIGATOR

For younger Readers

THE AIR-RAID SHELTER
FANNY WITCH GOES SPIKKY SPOO!
FANNY WITCH & THUNDER LIZARD

The Karate Princess and the Cut-throat Robbers

Jeremy Strong

Illustrated by Simone Abel

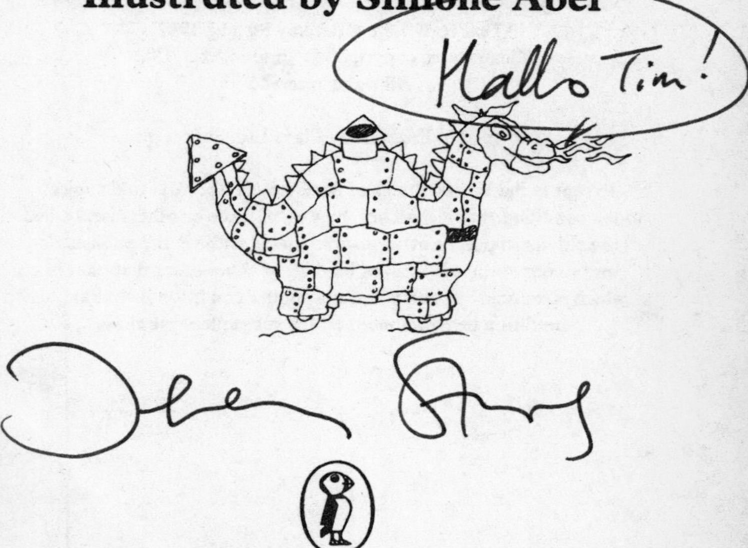

PUFFIN BOOKS

With many thanks to Joy and Ivo and, of course, to Linbeck

PUFFIN BOOKS

Published by the Penguin Group
Penguin Books Ltd, 27 Wrights Lane, London W8 5TZ, England
Penguin Books USA Inc., 375 Hudson Street, New York, New York 10014, USA
Penguin Books Australia Ltd, Ringwood, Victoria, Australia
Penguin Books Canada Ltd, 10 Alcorn Avenue, Toronto, Ontario, Canada M4V 3B2
Penguin Books (NZ) Ltd, 182–190 Wairau Road, Auckland 10, New Zealand

Penguin Books Ltd, Registered Offices: Harmondsworth, Middlesex, England

First published by A & C Black (Publishers) Ltd 1989
Published in Puffin Books 1991
3 5 7 9 10 8 6 4

Printed in England by Clays Ltd, St Ives plc

I

A Birthday Note

'Haaa-wak!' Splinters of wood flew in the air. A thick tree trunk broke in half and toppled to the ground. The huge, hairy ape-like monster that had just chopped the log with one swift blow of his bare hand looked up and grinned. Several of his sharp black teeth showed.

'How was that, Highship?' growled the Bogle, scratching his powerful chest with some very long finger-nails.

The Princess Belinda, sitting with her back against a wall, lazily opened one eye and groaned. 'Knackerleevee, I have told you a thousand times not to call me anything like that. My name is Belinda. Anyhow, I'm getting bored. Ever since I rescued you from The Marsh At The End Of The World and taught you karate you've done nothing but chop up bits of wood all over the place.'

Knackerleevee's muscle-bound shoulders drooped pathetically. 'Just one more,' he pleaded. 'Go on – please?'

'Oh all right, but only one.'

The Bogle perked up and his pink eyes sparkled. 'Just watch, Your Royalness!' The hairy creature turned and plodded off through the trees. The crunch of his giant steps faded away until Belinda could hear nothing. She waited, listening and watching intently. Nothing. She got to her feet and peered towards the trees.

At last there came a distant crashing, getting louder and louder until the great Bogle burst from the woods and thundered across the grass. 'Aaaaaaaaaaaaaa – HA!!'

Knackerleevee suddenly launched his whole flailing body into the air, sailed inelegantly over Belinda's astonished head and delivered a shattering blow with his heel to the ancient brick wall behind her. Bricks spilled every whichway and the Bogle fell with an earth-shaking thud on his back. He glanced up at Belinda and grinned.

'Very impressive,' she said. 'I was enjoying leaning against that.' She shook brick dust out of her short dark hair. 'This place now looks like a builder's yard. Sometimes I wonder if I did the right thing teaching you how to do karate.' The little princess sighed deeply and kicked half-heartedly at a brick. 'Oh I'm so bored. Isn't there anything exciting to do? What's our friend Hubert up to? Still working on his mystery painting that he won't let anyone see?'

Knackerleevee scrambled to his feet and lumbered after Belinda. 'I haven't seen him for days. He's a strange one.'

Again Belinda sighed. 'I wish I could paint. At least I'd be occupied. There doesn't seem much for a princess to do these days, especially one that can only do karate. I think I must be unemployed. You know Knackerleevee, I miss the old days – all that trouble and adventure. When I set off to capture you and I thought I was going to marry Prince Bruno de Bruno Bunkum Krust I wasn't bored at all. My heart was always pounding – there were Cut-throat Robbers to fight and that wicked Saramanda Sneak . . .' Belinda gave a giggle. 'I wonder what Bruno and Saramanda are up to now. She'd do anything to get her hands on diamonds, especially if they were somebody else's. I can't imagine them being married. She was so cunning and he was just a hunk of beefcake, all muscles and no brains.'

'Like me,' murmured Knackerleevee, staring dolefully at the ground. 'That's what I am, all muscle and stupid.'

Belinda smiled and put one arm as far round him as she could reach – which wasn't all that far. 'I have to admit he was more handsome than you, but he certainly wasn't nearly so hairy. Anyway, there's one thing about you that Bruno never had.'

The Bogle sniffed and shuffled his feet. 'What?' he croaked.

Belinda gave him a squeeze. 'You care about things. You care about people, which is a great deal more than Bruno or Saramanda do. That's worth a lot. Look, there's Hubert, painting under that tree. Ssssh – let's creep up and see what his amazing secret picture is all about!'

The two friends tiptoed up behind the Royal Artist and peered over his shoulders. Belinda frowned. Knackerleevee screwed up his eyes until they almost vanished beneath his shaggy eyebrows. He tilted his big head to one side to get a different angle on the painting. Belinda gave a polite little cough.

'Neargh!' Hubert almost jumped out of his skin. His paint brush flew into the air, turned several excited somersaults and came down gracefully on Belinda's nose, leaving a little streak of bright blue. She was about to rub it off when Hubert suddenly recovered from his shock and gripped her hands.

'No! Leave it – that's it! I've got it! I've got it!' The artist danced up and down in his excitement. 'For weeks I've been trying to find the right blue.'

He seized his palette and mixed paints furiously, while the Bogle picked up the canvas Hubert had been working on and turned it slowly round and round. He could make no sense of it whatsoever. It just looked like a load of different coloured blue splodges.

'Clouds? No. Water? No. Cotton-wool balls?' Knackerleevee muttered. 'No. I give up.' He thrust the canvas under Hubert's nose. 'What is it?'

Hubert stopped mixing colours and his face reddened.

'Well, go on,' said Belinda encouragingly. 'You've made such a fuss about it, and here I am standing like a lemon with a blue splodge on my nose – what on earth is it?'

'It's just that . . . well . . . what I've . . . you see . . . it's the same blue as your eyes,' he said in a rush at last, going even redder, if that were possible.

The Princess Belinda looked at Hubert, at the palette, and then at the painting. 'You've spent all this time trying to find the right blue to match my eyes?' she murmured.

'They are a rather extraordinary blue,' Hubert pointed out. Now it was Belinda's turn to blush, just a fraction. She took the canvas from Knackerleevee's clumsy grip and carefully placed it back on the easel. Glancing thoughtfully at Hubert, she asked if she could please wipe the smudge off her nose now?

Hubert hastily handed her his paint rag and Belinda wiped off the blue smudge and left a red one there instead. Hubert gave an apologetic little cough and carefully wiped it off for her.

'Oh – thank you.'

They both stared at their feet with embarrassment. Knackerleevee stared down too, thinking some kind of foot inspection must be taking place. 'Are my toe-nails dirty?' he asked gruffly.

Belinda laughed. 'No, it's all right, my big Bogle beasty. Listen, I've just remembered that it's my mum's birthday tomorrow . . .'

'You mean the Queen's birthday?' interrupted Hubert.

'Yes, my mum. I thought Knackerleevee and I

could bake a cake – you know he's a dab hand at sponges, and I can do the icing. I was wondering what to give her and then I remembered we've got that diamond mine on the other side of the Deep Dark Forest haven't we? You've got a good eye for beautiful things Hubert, so you nip down to the mine and find her a nice diamond stone while we bake the cake, and we'll meet you at my mum and dad's place.'

'You mean the palace?' Hubert asked.

'Well that is where they live.'

Knackerleevee was waving his arms up and down with great excitement. 'Can I really bake a cake for your mum – sorry – I mean her Really Royal Highwhatsitness?'

'Yes,' laughed Belinda. 'Now let's get on with it.'

Hubert put down his paint brush and set off immediately for the diamond mine, while Belinda and the Bogle went into the kitchen and made busy with the birthday cake. By the time they had finished the cake looked splendid and there was sponge mix and icing all over the floor, walls and ceiling. They wrapped the still warm cake in paper, saddled up a couple of horses (Knackerleevee's mount was an extra-large, extra-strong shire horse) and rode over to Belinda's parents' place.

Belinda's mother was a tall, elegant woman with a peaceful nature, quite the opposite of her husband. She was sitting on the croquet lawn in a deckchair when Belinda and Knackerleevee arrived.

'Happy Birthday!' shouted the Bogle. 'How old are you?'

Belinda rolled her eyes in despair at ever teaching him any manners, but the Queen didn't seem to mind.

'I'm twenty-nine,' she said gracefully.

'Twenty-nine last year,' grunted King Stormbelly, as he waddled down the steps to the lawn and gave his daughter a peck of a kiss on her cheek. 'Don't look at me like that, you Bogle beast – I'm not going to kiss you for all the tea in China!'

'Hallo Daddy,' smiled Belinda. 'Isn't it a lovely day?'

'Depends on what you mean by lovely,' he snapped. 'I've got a headache, you're still not married and the cat's got fleas. Things could be better.'

Belinda brought out the cake. 'Perhaps this will cheer you up. Look, Knackerleevee has made Mum a cake for her birthday.'

The Queen clapped her hands. 'It's beautiful, Knackerleevee. Thank you – and if the King won't kiss you, I will.'

Bogle's don't really blush, they just sort of go soggy at the knees, and that's exactly what Knackerleevee did.

At this point there was a tremendous disturbance at the palace gate. Someone burst past the guards and came running towards them.

'Who on earth can that be?' demanded King Stormbelly crossly. 'Did you invite anyone?'

'I think it's Hubert,' said Belinda. 'But he looks very upset. I wonder what's been going on.'

It was Hubert. He ran across the lawn and collapsed, breathless, at their feet, holding out a piece of crumpled paper in one hand. Belinda took the paper and carefully smoothed it out. On one side, in very big letters there was a message.

WE aRe hOLdiN HoobUrt 2 RAnsOm
IF YOu wanT 2 SeE Him AliVe Agen
Yu MUsT hand oVEr tHE DimONd MINe
Or tHE Big drAGOn WIlL gET Yu.

2

The Dragon

Belinda read through the note and handed it to her mother. The queen glanced at it and passed it on to her husband. Stormbelly read it, cursed, stamped a foot and then tried to kick one of the guards, which was always a sign that he was very angry.

But Belinda was quite amused. 'There can't be many people who would be silly enough to hold someone to ransom and then use their prisoner to deliver the ransom note. I mean, how ridiculous. It's just the sort of daft thing Saramanda's band of Cut-throat Robbers would do. Well, well, just when I thought life was boring. We shall have to find out about this. Come on Hubert, hurry up and get your breath back. Then you can tell us all about it.'

'I shall have to be quick,' panted the artist. 'Those horrible robbers are expecting me back.'

Belinda laughed. 'Silly twits. Tell me, did one of them have an enormous hat and swords stuffed down his boots?'

'That was the one who wrote the note!' shouted Hubert. 'He was awfully fierce. He kept waving his sword about – almost had my ears off a couple of times.'

'I bet Saramanda is behind all this,' mused

Belinda. 'Then what happened?'

'It was a bit odd really. First of all they tied me to a tree – not very well mind you. One of the robbers had to put his finger on the knot before they finished. They said the diamond mine was theirs by order, and if you didn't hand it over they'd chop me up into little bits and feed me to the dragon.'

'What dragon? Did you see it?'

'You poor thing,' murmured the Queen. 'You must have been terrified.'

Knackerleevee growled restlessly. 'Smash 'em and bash 'em and eat them for supper!' he suggested.

But Hubert wasn't listening. 'I didn't see the dragon, but I heard it huffing and letting off steam. It sounded frightful.'

'Hmmm, I bet there isn't a real dragon at all. They just said that to frighten you. Then what?'

'Well, the Robber Chief wrote that note and then decided they would have to send me with it because I was the only one who knew where you were. So they untied me. It's all been a bit of a strain. I'm not used to this kind of excitement.'

The Queen stood up hastily and offered her deckchair to Hubert, who collapsed into it gratefully.

King Stormbelly was marching round and round the lawn muttering angrily and tripping over the croquet hoops. 'Robbers and dragons! Can't have that! Against the law! Never heard of such a thing! What? Oh yes I have, yes I have!'

The King came waddling towards them, almost purple with rage. This is a repeat. Heard this story before – it's a . . . OW!' He caught his foot on another croquet hoop and fell flat on his face. Knackerleevee lifted him to his feet with one hand. 'Wretched things, fancy leaving them lying around like that.'

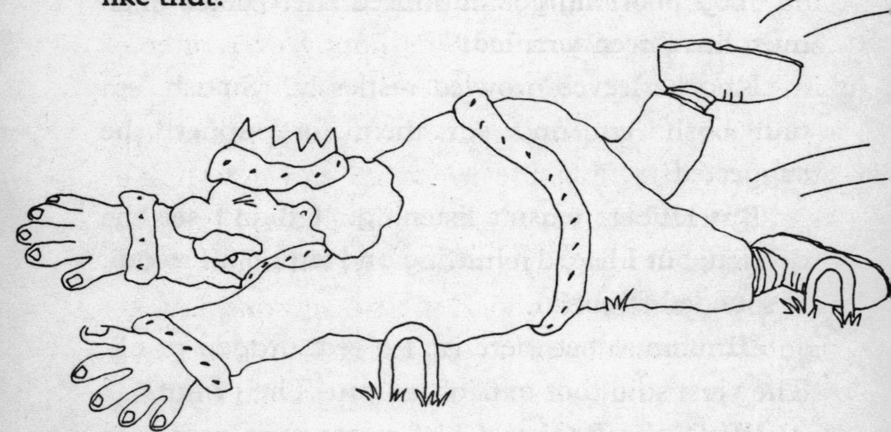

'What have you heard before, Dear?' asked the Queen calmly, brushing dirt from her husband's royal gown.

'Robbers and dragons! Fire-breathing dragons! Read about it in the paper this morning. They've been all over the place, demanding ransoms and diamonds and things like that. Terrible – eating princesses and everything.'

Belinda and the Queen looked at each other. Knackerleevee was already practising karate blows and mumbling to himself. 'We'll get 'em, we'll get 'em.'

Hubert lay in the deckchair and groaned.

'I wonder what we should do about it,' said Belinda, knowing full well what she intended.

'There's only one thing to do,' snapped Stormbelly. 'You have to offer your hand in marriage and half the kingdom as a reward for killing the dragon. Along comes some smart prince and saves the lot of you and it's happy ever after – isn't it?'

'No Daddy, it isn't. Look what happened last time. Anyhow, I *am* the princess. I only have half a kingdom, and much as you would like it, I have no wish to be married at present. The best thing is for me, Knackerleevee and Hubert to go and investigate. I'm sure there isn't a dragon. That's simply a scare tactic, but we shall certainly go and find out what *is* going on.'

'Fine, fine,' grunted King Stormbelly. 'Don't ask me for advice. You go off and get yourselves killed. See if I care.' The King turned on his heels, tripped on another hoop and fell.

Belinda helped him up, gave him a quick hug and then set off with her two friends. 'Don't worry Daddy, we'll be all right.'

Stormbelly watched her go. 'How come I had fifteen beautiful, talented and wonderfully normal daughters and then *her*?'

'Surely it's because she's different that you love her more than the others?' suggested the Queen teasingly.

'Me? Love her more... Pish! Rubbish! Stupid girl's only going to get herself frazzled by some loony dragon – huh!' The King stamped off to the castle, carefully avoiding the croquet hoops.

Hubert was not at all happy about returning to the diamond mine. He had a strong feeling that his ears were in grave danger. On the other hand Knackerleevee couldn't wait to get to grips with the Cut-throat Robbers. He'd met them before and it was all Belinda could do to keep him quiet.

'We must creep up on them and take them by surprise,' she kept saying. 'You sound like a herd of hippo frightened by a jellyfish.'

'Sorry Your Belindaness,' growled the Bogle.

The Princess suppressed a giggle and they pushed on.

At length, they left the Deep Dark Forest and reached rockier ground. Belinda crept forward, with the others close behind. The sound of voices ahead grew louder as the three approached a massive boulder. Taking great care, Belinda peered round the edge.

There were perhaps thirty robbers round the entrance to the mine, and a right scruffy lot they were too. Belinda quickly picked out the chief. His hat was by far the largest. It had an enormous brim that bounced up and down as he walked. Every so often it collapsed completely about his head, so that it looked more like an upturned bucket with a feather than anything else. Then the chief would flick the brim back into place and utter a foul curse. He rolled his eyes, spat at the ground, missed and hit his own shoe.

Belinda slid out of sight and whispered to her companions. 'There are only thirty of them, and that's my diamond mine they're guarding. What do you think?'

'I think we ought to go home,' muttered Hubert. 'I haven't made my will yet, nor got clean underwear on.'

'Let's get 'em!' growled the Bogle.

'Just what I think. Hubert, you'd better stay here. If there is trouble, you can get clear and warn the others. Here we go then, over the top. One, two, three, HAAAAAAAAA!'

The Princess and Knackerleevee leapt over the rock and landed facing the Cut-throat Robbers. Seven of them fell over with surprise, eight ran to the nearest trees and began climbing because they'd fought Belinda before and they didn't want another trip to hospital, and that left fifteen ready for a fight.

The Chief fished about in his boots for his biggest sword and slashed the air. Swish! Swash! it went. 'Ha!' he cried.

'Ha ha!' echoed Belinda.

'Huh!' grunted Knackerleevee.

The Robber Chief whirled his sword round and round and stepped towards Belinda. 'Ha! Take that! And that!'

Belinda watched him calmly. 'I see you've got spit on your boots again,' she said.

'What?' The Chief stopped and bent down to look. Belinda took good aim for a kick. 'Ow! Hey, that's cheating!' yelled the Chief. 'Come on you lot, there's only two of them.'

The robbers began to close in a circle round the pair. Their swords and knives glittered in the sunlight. Eventually one of the robbers was braver (or

more stupid) than the rest and he threw himself at Belinda. A moment later he was on his back in the dust, feeling as if he'd just run headlong into a brick wall. The Karate Princess rubbed her hands together.

'Anyone for second helpings?' she asked with a grin.

Three robbers had a quick mutter and made a dash at Knackerleevee. His huge hairy arms went biff! and baff! and three robbers lay unconscious in a neat pile on the ground. The rest of the band were beginning to get scared and back away, but their Chief snarled and growled at them, desperately trying to keep his hat straight, and the brim stiff.

'You may think you're winning princess,' he said scowling, 'but we've got a dragon and you won't be able to chop that up like firewood.'

Belinda began to laugh. 'You can't fool me. I know what you're up to. This is *my* diamond mine and it is *my* kingdom and you're not getting away with this. Your exploits have come to an end, so throw down your weapons before Knackerleevee and I do some real damage.'

At that moment, there was a hissing roar from the mouth of the mine. Knackerleevee stuffed his hairy fingers in his equally hairy ears. A huge belch of smoke drifted from the cave mouth. There was a long flash of flame and a glowing snout appeared, long and shiny. Then a pair of glittering eyes stared out. Slowly an immense and fearsome creature hauled itself from the mine, belching smoke and flame and snorting like an angry rhinoceros.

Knackerleevee and Belinda stood, transfixed, whilst the Robber Chief bellowed with laughter. But Belinda had just seen someone else, a tall and very beautiful young woman with radiantly golden hair down to her waist, and an utterly charming smile.

'Well, if it isn't the Princess Saramanda Sneak,' murmured Belinda, quickly glancing round for the princess's husband, Bruno de Bruno. He was nowhere to be seen, which was a bit puzzling.

'And if it isn't the Princess Belinda,' crowed Saramanda. 'At last my moment has come. Ever since you took *my* half of the kingdom I've been waiting to get even with you. You took the diamond mine that should have been mine, and now I've got it back, but I'm not going to stop here. I'm just on my way to your father's palace – I quite fancy living in style!'

The Robber Chief stepped forward with his sword. 'Shall I chop their heads off, Your Highness?'

'No, no, not yet. They may come in useful. Take them away and put them somewhere safe, where they cannot possibly escape. I know just the place. Take them to The Tower With A Million Steps – no one ever escapes alive from there.'

The dragon gave another belch of flame that almost burnt the hairs off Knackerleevee's toes. Belinda just had time to think that her poor mother was going to have a rotten birthday, then she found herself trussed up and tied to a pole. The robbers carried her and the Bogle away with much cackling and dancing, while Hubert lay behind his rock in a state of shock.

3

What's To Be Done Now?

The sun was setting over the distant mountains before Hubert could pluck up enough courage to open one eye and take a little peek around the rock. The robbers had long since departed, with the great dragon clanking and hissing behind them. Saramanda had mounted her milk-white charger and galloped off into the sunset with her golden hair streaming out behind her.

Hubert opened his other eye and stood up, carefully placing his knees together so that they'd stop each other from shaking quite so much. This was a terrible business – quite, quite terrible. He must alert Belinda's parents. They'd know what to do. He cast one more worried look around to check that he wasn't about to be pounced on by thirty Cut-throat Robbers and several tons of hot dragon, then set off as fast as he could for King Stormbelly's palace.

He arrived puffing and panting, just as he had done when he'd delivered the first message. The King paced up and down, impatiently waiting for the poor artist to get his breath back. The Queen was altogether more useful and fetched Hubert a glass of water and a chocolate biscuit.

'Come on, come on,' rasped Stormbelly. 'Spit it out man!'

Hubert looked a trifle surprised, but dutifully spat the biscuit out on to the best Persian carpet. 'Not the biscuit you stupid fellow! What's the message this time?'

'They've got the princess and Knackerleevee. It was Saramanda and her robbers. There really is a dragon – huge, monstrous, and breathing fire. They've taken the princess away and locked her up in The Tower With A Million Steps.'

'The Tower With A Million Steps? They can't do that. It's against the law!' King Stormbelly turned to the Queen, red with anger. 'That's against the law isn't it?'

'Yes dear, I'm certain it is, but . . .'

'That's it then. I'm going after them. I won't let them get away with kidnapping my own daughter – even if she has got a squitty nose. Army? Army? Where are you? Come on out wherever you are! This is an emergency.'

Stormbelly shouted and bellowed and marched up and down waving a walking stick and practising salutes. 'They're never there when you want them. Come on, come on!' he bawled, as soldiers began to pile into the living room from every direction.

They were pulling on vests and leggings and thick leather boots, struggling into massive iron breastplates, just a touch too rusty, and hurriedly trying to clear their gun barrels of all the sticky sweet papers they'd hidden down them every time they were caught chewing on sentry duty.

By this stage the room was packed with soldiers of every size, shape and description, including the General, who was attempting to squeeze himself and his horse through the french windows. The Queen had, of course, quietly disappeared to another, calmer room, taking the still-shaken Hubert with her.

Now King Stormbelly clambered on to a huge oak sideboard in an attempt to make himself seen and heard better. 'Right men, all eyes this way, attention! ATTENTION!'

Seventy-eight soldiers tried to salute at one and the same time, jamming fingers and elbows into each other as they did so. A few minor fights broke out.

'You did that on purpose . . .'

'No, I didn't. It was his fault . . .'

'Get your finger out of my nose!'

'That's not my finger – THIS is my finger, in your ear . . .'

'That's enough! ENOUGH! STOP!' screeched King Stormbelly, but the noise grew steadily louder and louder, until at last the General forced his way into the room, horse and all, drew his pistol and fired it in the air. There was an almighty crash as the big chandelier fell from the ceiling, trapping half a dozen soldiers beneath it. Everyone stopped and looked expectantly at the General. He, in turn, looked very embarrassed and waved his pistol at the King.

'Right men,' began Stormbelly. 'My daugher, the Princess Belinda, has been taken prisoner.'

'Shame,' murmured the soldiers.

'Exactly – and we're going to rescue her!'

'Hurrah!'

'Quite right too. All we have to do is overcome some silly old fire-breathing dragon . . .'

'Come on lads, we ought to get back home. It's past our bed-time . . .'

'STOP! There's a reward for all of you if we succeed,' continued the King, with a crafty look in his eyes. 'Jelly Babies all round – now, how about it?'

The General stared thoughtfully at the ceiling and muttered into his white moustache. Stormbelly glared at him angrily.

'All right, an extra packet of toffees for General Fitzenstartz,' he added with great generosity. The General gave a big smile, drew his sword, waved it bravely a couple of times, reducing the curtains to shreds, and shouted to his men.

'Come on men – to battle!'

'To battle!' cried the seventy-eight soldiers, and they trooped out of the living room and across the croquet lawn. Only seventeen tripped over, and one had to stay behind and have a sticking plaster put on his knee by the Queen. The soldiers marched off into The Deep Dark Forest.

The Queen stood at her bedroom window with Hubert and watched the army depart. She heaved a long sigh. 'My birthday started off so well,' she murmured. 'I don't know what went wrong. Oh well, let's go and have a cup of tea while we're waiting. Look at my silly husband – off to war and he's left his toothbrush behind.'

Meanwhile, what was happening to Belinda and Knackerleevee? They had been carried for mile after mile, bouncing up and down very uncomfortably on their poles like a pair of trapped tigers, until they had at last reached The Tower With A Million Steps. There it was, climbing into the sky to a staggering height. Well and truly staggering once you tried climbing all those steps.

It was a square tower, but inside it had a circular, spiral staircase. Nobody had ever discovered why there was this difference between the outside and the inside, because the architect had died of Immense Laughing Madness before he could explain.

The Robber Chief banged five times on the enormous door. For the next fifteen minutes bolts were pulled back, padlocks opened, chains taken off, and keys turned and twisted until at length the thick wooden doors were pulled back and the Cut-throat Robbers marched in with their two prisoners.

The Robber Chief seized a horn and gave five echoing blasts. He looked up towards the terrible top of the tower. Nothing happened. He blew on the horn again and turned to his deputy. 'There's never a lift when you want one. I suppose it's out of order again.'

But then there came a creaking and squeaking from above, and out of the gloomy darkness a large basket-like affair appeared, slowly twisting and turning on the end of a thick rope. Down it came until at last it touched the ground with a soft thump.

'Thank goodness for that,' breathed the Robber Chief. 'I couldn't face all those steps at my age.'

His deputy turned a puzzled face towards the Chief. 'Why? How old are you? Ouch!' He got a swift slap for being personal.

Belinda began to wriggle and squirm, but she was tied up much too firmly, and in a moment she was cast into the lift-basket like a bag of dirty laundry. It took eleven robbers to get Knackerleevee safely in. Not only did he struggle, but he was extraordinarily heavy. The robbers had managed to tie a gag round his mouth, so all he could do was growl and dig his elbows into his captors.

'Well, well, well, most royal princess,' smirked the Chief. 'Now we've got you just where we want you. Once you get to the top of this tower, there's no escape. You see, the stairs stop half-way up. There's only the lift, and that's operated from the top of the stairs. So once you're at the top, there's no way down, because the lift will be taken away.'

He began to laugh so much that the brim of his hat collapsed over his face. 'Who put the lights out?' he shouted, then flicked the brim up once more, narrowed his eyes and tried to look doubly fierce. 'Meanwhile, me and the lads here, we're going to take over your Pa's castle and all the diamonds in the entire kingdom!'

'You'll never get away with this,' said Belinda, as the basket gave a lurch and lifted clear of the floor.

The Robber Chief doffed his hat and gave a sweeping bow. 'Goodbye your Highness! Goodbye!' All the other robbers lifted their hats in turn and chanted teasingly. 'Bye bye Your Majesty!' Then they all fell about laughing, while the lift slowly creaked up the tower on its long journey into the gloom.

As the basket swayed upwards Belinda struggled into a sitting position, leaning against Knackerleevee's hairy body. She looked up at the Bogle's face, half hidden by the large gag across his mouth.

'Are you all right?' she asked quietly. The huge creature nodded.

'I'm sorry about the mess we're in, Knackerleevee, I really am.' The Bogle moved his head from one side to the other as if to say it didn't matter.

'We'll find a way out, don't you worry,' muttered the princess, but Knackerleevee's pink eyes reflected all the despair and feeling of hopelessness that filled his great heart.

4

The Tower With A Million Steps

High above the swaying basket, hidden pulleys creaked and squeaked like a geriatric rookery. Belinda stared into the gloom. Soon she could not even hear the robbers' laughter far below. She could faintly make out the thick walls of the tower and the spiral stairs climbing endlessly, until suddenly they did end, on a large flat space.

Bolted firmly to this platform was a massive piece of wooden machinery, its cogs, wheels, pulleys and levers all grinding slowly round and round, up and down, and backwards and forwards, as two huge men almost as big as Knackerleevee, turned a handle that was slowly winding the lift-basket to the top of the tower. Their muscles bulged and they turned their dark, scowling faces upon the basket as it passed, and leered at the two prisoners. A moment later they returned, sweating, to their task and the basket carried on upwards.

For another fifteen minutes the lift ascended in a series of jerks and jolts. Belinda was glad that she could no longer see the ground – the mere thought that she was so high sent little shivers scurrying down her spine like a trickle of crushed ice. Light began to fill the tower. At first it was just a glimmer, but it grew steadily until the princess could see each brick in the wall quite clearly.

Her heart gave a leap of joy as she heard voices above – there were people at the top! Maybe they could help! Looking up she saw another platform. Arms were stretched towards her, hands waving, and every now and then a young face peered down anxiously. Belinda yelled up the shaft. 'Hallo up there – hallo!'

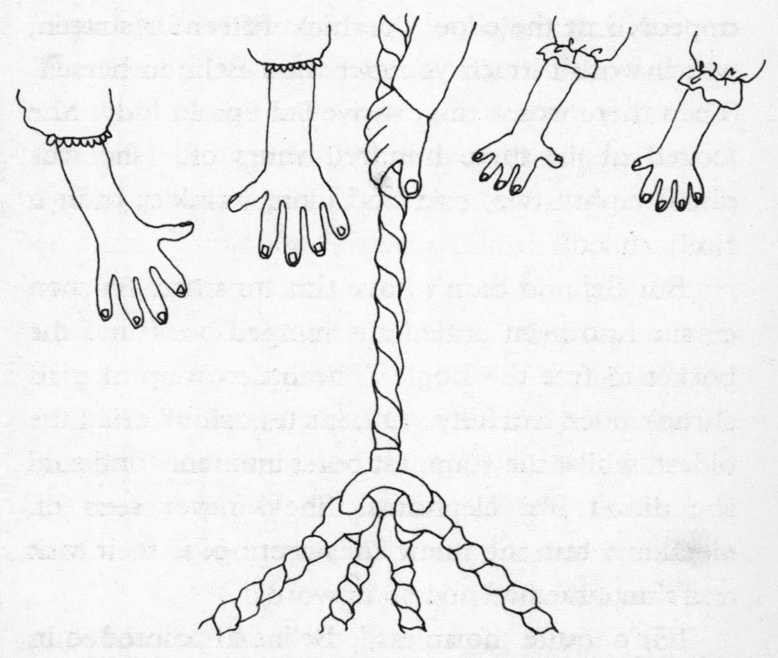

There was a lot of whispering and scurrying about at the edge of the platform. A girl of about fifteen with a dark, pretty face appeared. 'Who are you?' she cried. Belinda shouted back the answer. It was met with a chorus of groans.

Then the basket was bumping against the side of the platform and it stopped. Hands reached in and pulled Belinda out, but when they saw Knackerleevee, staring wild-eyed and shaking his huge hairy head at them, everyone drew back in fright.

Princess Belinda gazed at the little crowd with some amazement. There were nine girls, some only six or seven, the oldest – the one who had first appeared at the edge – perhaps fifteen or sixteen, which wasn't much younger than Belinda herself. Then there was a tiny, shrivelled up old lady. She looked about three hundred years old (she was about eighty-two) and had more wrinkles than a rhubarb leaf.

But Belinda didn't have time to stare. As soon as she had been untied she jumped back into the basket to free the Bogle. The little group of girls shrank back fearfully. 'Oh, it's a gorilla!' cried the oldest, whilst the youngest burst into tears and said she didn't like elephants. She'd never seen an elephant, but she knew they were big, so it was quite an educated guess.

'He's quite harmless,' Belinda pointed out, removing the gag. 'He's a Bogle from The Marsh At The End Of The World, and he is a great friend of mine.'

The old lady's twinkling eyes widened and she hurried forward with quick, duck-like steps. 'A bogle you say? Well, well, you must be the famous Princess Belinda – The Karate Princess that I've heard so much about. Hmmmm – and this is a real Bogle?' She went across to Knackerleevee and stroked his hairy arm, peering up into Knackerleevee's puzzled face. 'What do you feed him on?'

Knackerleevee opened his huge mouth, showing all his sharp black teeth. 'People sandwiches is what I like best, but since I've been with the Princess here I've stuck to sausage rolls and doughnuts.'

'But who are you?' demanded Belinda of the old lady. 'Who are all these girls? Where did they come from? Can we escape? Is there a way down?'

The old lady gave Belinda a gummy smile, took her by the elbow and guided her to an old sofa, which had most of its stuffing spilling on to the stone floor. As they sat down, a rat scampered hurriedly out of the way in case it got mistaken for a cushion.

'Well my dear, I'm not sure where to start. First of all, let's see, you must have been captured by the Princess Saramanda – hmmm! No wonder she wants to get rid of you! Hmmm, pity that she's got you here but never mind, we'll do something about that later.'

'What do you mean we'll do something about it later?' demanded Belinda.

'You wait a moment,' nodded the old lady. 'And we've got the Bogle here too. Hmmm, well, that's a bit of a problem. Still, who knows?'

'Who knows what?' cried Belinda with ever-increasing frustration.

'Well, yes, hmmm, don't fret now,' mused the old lady, her bright hazel-nut eyes shining amongst the wealth of wrinkles on her face.

'Now, as for all these young girls – scared as rabbits in a stewpot they are – all princesses of course. They're supposed to have been eaten by the dragon but naturally *he* doesn't eat much at all! Well, he wouldn't, would he?'

'Why not?' asked Belinda, curiously.

'Why not? Hmmm, well, all in due course. Don't hurry me. Where was I? Yes – they're all princesses captured by the terrible dragon. Ha, ha . . .' The old lady began to laugh quietly, then stopped abruptly. 'Now, as for me, my name is Mulligatawny.'

Knackerleevee grunted hungrily.

'Mulligatawny?' he repeated.

Belinda said she thought Mulligatawny was a kind of soup.

'So it is, so it is, and I invented it, along with a lot of other things. Oh, I've invented dozens and dozens of things, just about everything there is – except for my wrinkles. They're a natural feature, so to speak. Anyhow, someone decided to call me Mulligatawny. I suppose, when you come to think about it, I was lucky they didn't call me Chicken Broth, or Pot Noodle.'

'Pot Noodles?' murmured Knackerleevee, his tongue half hanging out. He cast a longing eye at the princesses, still huddled in a corner.

'And are you a princess too?' asked Belinda doubtfully.

'Ha! Of course not. It's not like that at all. You see, dear, my problems started when I invented a pair of automatic nail scissors.'

Belinda was no longer certain that she was hearing things properly. Here she was, stuck at the top of The Tower With A Milion Steps, with nine princesses and an old lady who said her problem was all to do with automatic nail scissors.

Mulligatawny smacked her gums together. 'Now, let me finish. We're almost there. I invented this thing and the Princess Saramanda heard about it. So off I went to the palace and she asked, all nice and lovey-dovey, did I have any other inventions? So I showed her the soup, and the stay-sharp pencil and the puppy-clock . . .'

'Puppy-clock?'

'Like a cuckoo-clock, only it goes woof, woof,' Mulligatawny explained. 'Then she got me inventing things for the palace – remote control curtain pullers, a dish-washer, diamond cutting equipment etcetera. One day she came along, all sweetness and light, and asked if I could make a big dragon for some fancy-dress party or other. Well, I managed to build this monstrous thing – breathes fire and everything, but then you've met it haven't you? Hmmm, well, what you don't know is that the dragon is made of metal and powered by steam. That's where all the clanking and hissing comes from, and the fire. It's got a big boiler that runs on wood, and a driver too.'

Belinda leapt to her feet. 'Of course! I bet that's where Prince Bruno de Bruno Bunkum Krust has been all this time. I knew he must be somewhere close by.'

Mulligatawny paused for a moment. 'Well, hmmm, that's about the most of it. Saramanda shut me up here to get me out of the way. Of course, she doesn't want anyone to know the dragon isn't real. Now she's going all over the place with her Cut-throat Robbers pretending to eat princesses and collecting diamonds without any bother. I was hoping . . .' The old lady squinted up at Belinda. 'I was hoping you might rescue us, but now you're stuck up here too.'

Belinda walked to the edge of the platform and stared down into the dark pit. 'There must be a way down,' she muttered. 'There must.'

Knackerleevee growled and paced the platform with her, while the nine princesses shrank back against the far walls and clung to each other for support. Pretty useless, these princesses, aren't they? But they'd never been trained for this sort of situation you see. Don't worry, they come into their own later!

The Bogle lumbered over to a low door and tried to open it, but it was firmly locked and barred. Belinda asked where it went. Mulligatawny shrugged her scrawny shoulders. 'There's a parapet that runs round the top of the tower. There's no escape from there.'

But the Karate Princess was getting angry. She had been tied up, and locked up for far too long already. She felt she had to do something and she didn't much care what it was. She stared moodily at the door, thinking of the open air and sky beyond it.

'Knackerleevee!'

The Bogle shifted himself to the princess's side. 'What do you think?' asked Belinda, with just a hint of a smile. The great beast glared at the door.

'I think a flying heel-kick, Mighty One,' he growled.

'I shall stamp on your foot if you call me that again. Ready? One, two, three, Haaaaaaaaaa – KERRUNCH!' The pair launched themselves into the air and smashed their feet into the door. It exploded off the door frame and the two assailants went crashing through. Out went the door, over the parapet and down, down, down in an endless fall. Out through the doorway went Knackerleevee and Belinda, carried by their own weight. Straight over the parapet went Belinda, with a scream of fear, closely followed by Knackerleevee.

The Bogle just managed to grab the top of the parapet with one hairy hand as he spilled over the edge and clung there, with the breath knocked from his body. Belinda clutched frantically at his right ankle with both her small hands, her legs swinging wildly in space. She glanced down and hurriedly screwed up her eyes as tightly as possible. Somewhere, miles below, the ground swam round and round. She could still see the wooden door, a tiny revolving speck far beneath her, twisting and turning on its journey down.

5

To The Rescue

Belinda screamed desperately at the Bogle. 'Hang on, Knackerleevee, hang on!'

'I am hanging on Highlindaship,' he shouted back hoarsely. 'I'm not *that* stupid!'

Mulligatawny peered anxiously over the edge at the two friends. 'Hmmm, well, oh dear – would you like some help?' She got down on her knees and gripped Knackerleevee's wrist. The Bogle was surprised at how strong the little old lady's grasp was. He fished about in mid-air with the other hand until he found the top of the parapet. Then, bit by bit, he hauled himself and the princess back over the wall and on to the balcony. They both lay there panting and recovering from the shock.

'I didn't like that very much,' observed Belinda, crawling to the edge and looking down to check if it really was as far as she thought. It was – probably further in fact.

The truth of their situation filled her with despair. She felt so useless. She knew that any princess worth her salt would simply unravel half a mile of golden hair, chuck it over the side and wait for a handsome prince to climb up and rescue her. But not only was her hair black, it was short and curly.

And anyhow, she would much rather do all the rescuing herself.

But there appeared to be no way down from the tower. By now Saramanda and her Cut-throat Robbers had probably overrun the countryside for miles around. 'We've got to stop her somehow,' muttered Belinda.

Mulligatawny pottered out from the tower with some mugs of hot coffee and a few home-made biscuits. She sat herself down on an old chair and smiled a toothless smile.

'Don't give up too soon, princess. Of course, you know why Saramanda wants you out of the way, hmmmm? It's not simply for revenge. She knows that you and Knackerleevee are the only people left who can stop her getting her wicked ways. There is one other person though . . .'

'But who's that?' Belinda was surprised. She didn't know of any other karate expert like herself apart from the Bogle.

Mulligatawny gave a sly cackle. 'Why, me – of course!'

Knackerleevee burst out laughing straight into his coffee mug and coffee sprayed everywhere. The old lady wiped the front of her dress clean and sniffed.

'Hmmm, well, don't forget that I made that dragon. Very proud of that dragon I was; took a lot of inventing and what have you, and I can make other things too. It may interest you to know that I've got a little idea that may help to get one of you off this tower.'

Belinda jumped to her feet. 'Where is it? Let's go at once! Perhaps it's not too late to stop Saramanda and Bruno the dragon.'

'Just a moment dear,' insisted Mulligatawny, getting up and leading the princess into the tower. 'You can't go charging at this like you do with your karate. Look, this is what I've got in mind.'

She pulled an untidy heap of cloth and sticks from beneath her bed. With Belinda's help she dragged them out on to the balcony, where they lay in the sunshine. 'That,' said Mulligatawny with a smile, pointing at the pile, 'is your only chance of escape.'

Belinda sighed and pushed at the sticks with one foot. The old lady was obviously mad. Her brain was collapsing with old age. Belinda glanced across at Knackerleevee and rolled her eyes, but Mulligatawny caught the look and seized Belinda's arm with a scrawny grip of iron.

'I'm not as stupid as you think. Watch.' She began to lay out the sticks in some kind of pattern. Sometimes she poked one of them through a long length of cloth. Bits of string were tied on here and there, and slowly a weird geometric shape was laid out across the balcony floor. The cloth was pulled tighter and tighter until it looked like some very large, strangely twisted bedsheet, full of patches and holes. Hardly surprising – it used to be a bedsheet full of patches and holes.

'What on earth is it?' murmured Belinda, totally bewildered.

'A hang-glider,' said Mulligatawny.

'But what's a hang-glider?'

'Been inventing it ever since I got stuck up here by that Saramanda woman. Hmmm, well, there's only one way down from this tower and that's over the edge. Like a bird – fly!'

Belinda stared at the old woman. She swallowed hard. 'You mean I hold on to that and jump off the edge?'

Mulligatawny nodded.

Knackerleevee hid his face in his big hands and began to moan softly. Belinda took a quick look over the edge and almost fainted. She had been scared when she first faced the Bogle in The Marsh At The End Of The World, but that was nothing compared to the way she felt now. It was as if her entire insides had turned to jelly and dribbled out of the bottom of her jog-suit. At length she managed to crack a question. 'Has anyone ever tried this . . . this . . . thingy-glider?'

'You'll be the first dear,' said Mulligatawny. 'Think of the honour!'

'Think of the danger.'

'Imagine flying through the air like a real bird!'

'Or hitting the ground at one hundred and fifty miles an hour like a Major Accident. I haven't even got a crash-helmet!'

'Think of the glory!' insisted the old lady.

'What about the funeral? You'll need matchbox sized coffins for all my bits and pieces.'

The Princess Belinda gazed over the edge once more, then turned to Mulligatawny. 'Do you really think this thing will fly?'

The old lady paused a moment and then nodded. 'Quite probably.'

'And it's the only way down?'

'As far as I know.'

Belinda took a deep breath and closed her eyes. 'Then I'll give it a try,' she said very quickly, just in case she changed her mind half-way through the sentence. 'Show me what to do.'

Meanwhile, what was the wicked Saramanda doing? And where was King Stormbelly with his brave army of dashing men? Strange to tell, the two were about to meet on the plain of battle. From one direction came the Princess Saramanda, looking positively glorious on her white charger. Her dazzlingly long golden hair waved like a banner in the wind, and her clear blue eyes flashed evil thoughts as she mentally counted up all the diamonds she was about to own. Of course, her eyes are a quite different blue from Belinda's, as Hubert will quickly tell you if you ask him. There's no comparison at all.

Behind Saramanda came the Cut-throat Robbers. Their hats flopped and flapped as they rode and they kept changing direction because half the time they couldn't see where they were going. Then they'd curse their horses for being stupid, dig their heels into the flanks of the unfortunate creatures and hurry after their leader. They were armed to the teeth with really nasty swords, extra-sharp daggers, and a wide selection of pistols in full working order.

And behind the Cut-throat Robbers came the jangling dragon, with steam pouring from its back, because Bruno de Bruno had lifted the bonnet up to get some fresh air. It was a bit hot and clammy inside and even the wonderful Bruno could only take so much of his personal body odour, prince or not. There he was, as radiant and handsome as ever, his strong jaw strutting forward and not a single simple thought in his noble head.

As Saramanda reached the top of a suitably high hill she stopped and held up her hand. Behind, the robbers all cannoned into each other until they were mostly lying in an angry kicking heap on the grass. The dragon clattered up and down like some huge guard dog, checking that none of the robbers were having second thoughts about going to war and were trying to sneak back home.

Hardly had Saramanda's army taken up their position, when King Stormbelly breasted the hill on the other side of the plain. His seventy-eight soldiers fussed around him, brandishing some very

fierce weapons indeed. There were swords and pistols, knives, forks, spears, bows and arrows, scissors, a lawn-mower, boomerangs, a fishing-net, several extra-large soup ladles and half a dozen corkscrews.

General Fitzenstartz cantered forward on his horse, put a telescope to his eye the wrong way round and surveyed the enemy. 'Hah! They're all midgets Your Highness. They're absolutely tiny. She's got an army of dwarves and a dog. They won't give us any bother.' He snapped the telescope shut and turned to address the troops.

'This is a far, far better thing,' he began, 'far better – better by far than – than anything else!' he added with a grand gesture. 'We shall fight them on the beaches and fight them by the duckpond and fight them in our sleep if necessary, but we shall never, NEVER give in!'

There was silence.

'Hurrah!' cheered the General all by himself.

By this time King Stormbelly had managed to slide off his horse (deliberately) and unpack his deckchair. He carefully set it out facing the battle plain, blew up his inflatable cushion and sat down. 'Right you are,' he shouted to General Fitzenstartz. 'I'm ready. You can start now.'

The General drew his curving sword and waved it proudly in the sunshine. This was the sword his mother had given him for Christmas. It had, *To Binky, Love from Mum*, engraved on the handle.

'Death or Glory!' yelled the General. 'Charge!' And he and his horse plunged down the hillside at full gallop. The seventy-eight soldiers watched him go and turned to one another and began to natter quietly amongst themselves.

'Get himself chopped to bits if he's not careful.'

'What does he think he's playing at?'

'Soldiers, I think, but I could be wrong.'

King Stormbelly stood up impatiently. 'You're supposed to go with him you dimwits! Go on – get moving!'

The soldiers nudged each other, rolled their eyes, wearily picked up their weapons and trudged after General Fitzenstartz, who was now a distant speck, galloping across the plain towards Saramanda's waiting troops.

She watched the steady approach of General Fitzenstartz and almost fell of her horse laughing when she saw the little group of soldiers that eventually began to wander down the hill towards her.

'Bruno,' she called. 'I say, Bruno darling, do come and look at this. Such a shame. I was looking forward to a real battle, steel upon steel and a bit of blood and a few arms and legs lying about the place. But never mind, just wander down the hill Bruno and breathe on them a bit. That should do the trick. I think I'll sit and watch. Oh, what fun!'

6

Disaster Or Success?

From the cockpit of the great metal dragon Bruno de Bruno Bunkum Krust blew a kiss to his most beautiful, but utterly sneaky, wife. Then, he began to thrust bundles of firewood into the furnace beneath the dragon's boiler. Steam hissed from the pistons, the wheels began to turn and the dragon lurched off down the hill towards King Stormbelly's army, who were now wandering rather aimlessly across the plain.

General Fitzenstartz had by this time galloped straight up the far side, where, of course, he came face to face with Saramanda's Cut-throat Robbers, who were about to sit down to a nice cup of tea.

'Tally-ho!' yelled the brave general, and he charged straight through the robbers, taking great swipes with his sword which left many of their hat brims in absolute tatters. Then he was off like a whirlwind, out the other side and on and on until he disappeared from sight, still shouting 'CHAAAARGE!'

The robbers were seething. They stamped around complaining bitterly to each other and trying to get their hats knocked back into shape. 'Nobody told us war would be like this!' hissed the

Deputy Chief. 'He's gone and spilt all our milk now.'

'Stop snivelling and go and find a cow,' ordered the Chief, clouting his deputy round one ear.

Meanwhile, King Stormbelly's army had just begun to notice that a very noisy, very large, very fierce monster was clanking towards them. Occasional bursts of steam swirled from its sides in thick grey clouds, as Bruno de Bruno aimed the dragon at the very centre of the oncoming army. Just for effect he let out a spurt of flame and pulled on the whistle cord. A piercing shriek filled the air.

'It's a dragon!' screamed the front-line soldiers. 'Help! Save us!' In desperation they stopped on the spot, threw their weapons at the oncoming beast, turned tail and ran. 'Retreat! Sound the retreat!' they yelled as they made off back up the hill. Confusion reigned. The front-line soldiers ran into the middle-line rank and fell in a heap. The back-line men ran on to the heap and the dragon came nearer and nearer, with flames leaping from the snout.

'Eeek! squeaked one poor soldier, hurriedly emptying his water-bottle over his shoulder as flames heated his bottom.

'Run for your lives!' was the general cry that went up, as Stormbelly's army got back on their feet and raced up the hill.

The King watched the return of his troops with

a smug smile. He started to clap. 'Well done men! Defeated the rotters already? Good show! Good show! Jelly babies all . . .' His triumphant speech was cut short as he was knocked flying by the retreating army. Just as he managed to stumble to his feet, the steaming dragon appeared over the brow of the hill. Stormbelly paused and swallowed hard.

'Nice pussy, good pussy,' he murmured, backing away steadily. 'Good boy, come to daddy . . .'

Bruno de Bruno smiled to himself and yanked the whistle cord. Stormbelly let out a shriek that was even louder and took to his heels, rapidly overtaking his retreating army. 'Back to the palace!' he yelled. 'Take cover – last one in's a coward!' Even Stormbelly was rather puzzled by this last remark.

The King and his brave troops reached the palace in record time. But they had hardly crossed the drawbridge before the dragon and Saramanda's Cut-throat Robbers were there too. The battle was over. The robbers poured into the palace with whoops of delight, driving Stormbelly, the Queen and Hubert into the broom cupboard, where they hurriedly barricaded themselves in for safety.

Saramanda Sneak coolly sauntered up and down the great hall. She was joined by her prince, Bruno de Bruno, hot from the dragon.

'Well my sweet,' crooned the princess. 'I think that just about wraps it up. Not only do I have Belinda's half of the kingdom and her diamond mine, but now I've got her father's kingdom too.' She gave a momentary frown and sniffed through her delicate nostrils. 'Darling – I think you need a bath.'

The Princess Belinda stood on the edge of the parapet. Strapped about her small frame was Mulligatawny's strange thing of sheet and sticks. A cold wind pushed mockingly at the patchwork affair and a passing crow almost fell out of the sky laughing.

'I don't feel very confident,' murmured Belinda.

'It's fine,' insisted the old lady. 'Just as I planned.'

'Are you all right Belinda?' asked Knacker-leevee in a low growl.

The princess turned and smiled at him. 'You got my name right! You got it right for once!' The Bogle coloured slightly and lowered his eyes. Belinda bent down and whispered seriously in his ear for some time. A slow smile spread across the creature's face. He began to nod vigorously.

Mulligatawny tugged at Belinda's sleeve. 'Hmm, you know what to do when you land?'

'Up the million steps, overpower the two guards and get the lift-basket up to you.' Belinda paused and then added, 'You know, a million steps sounds an awful lot.'

'Go up in twos,' said the old lady. 'Then there'll be half as many.'

'You're too clever,' answered Belinda. She caught a glimpse of the ground far, far below and almost fainted. 'Let's hope you're clever enough to have got this hang-glider thing right.'

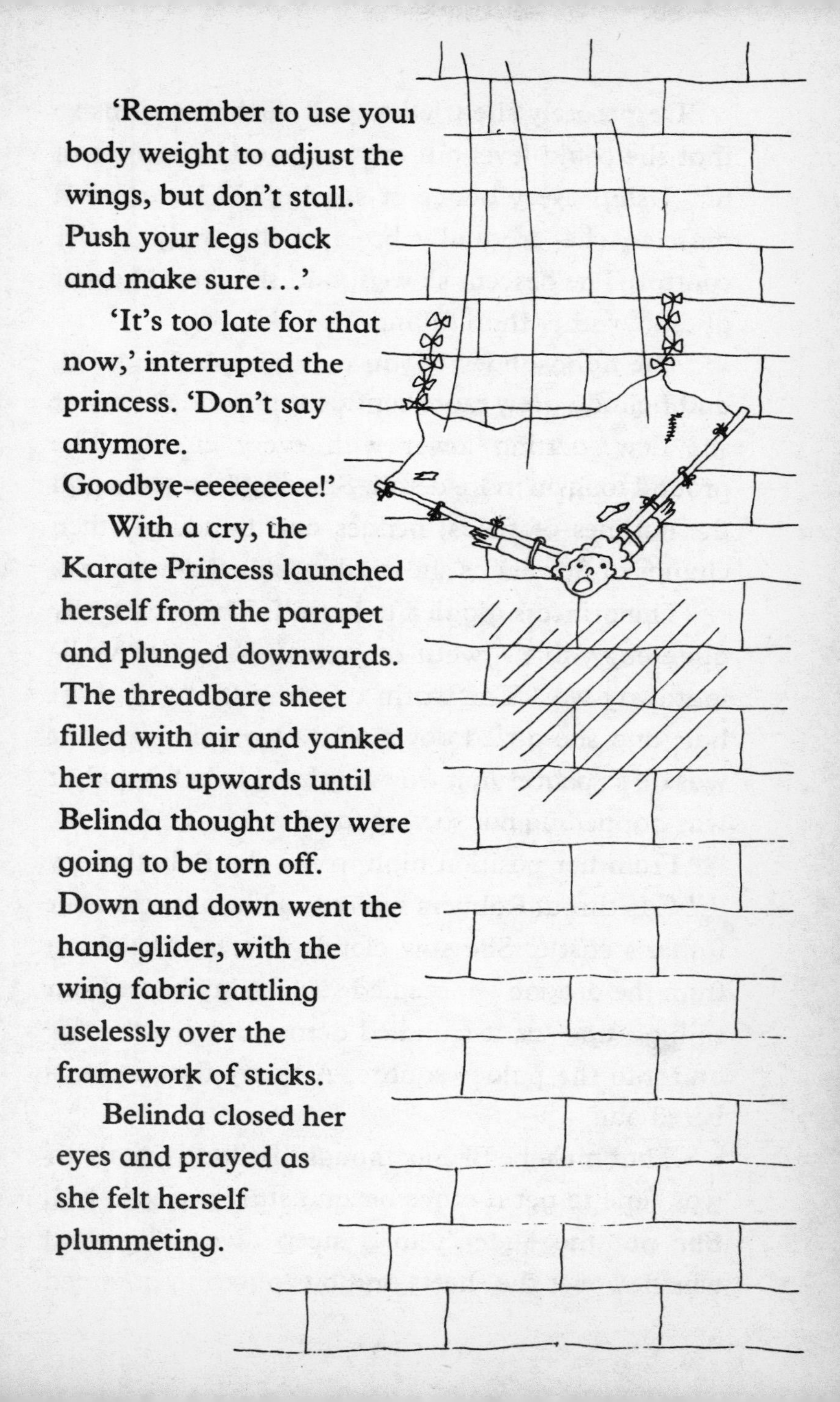

'Remember to use your body weight to adjust the wings, but don't stall. Push your legs back and make sure . . .'

'It's too late for that now,' interrupted the princess. 'Don't say anymore. Goodbye-eeeeeeeee!'

With a cry, the Karate Princess launched herself from the parapet and plunged downwards. The threadbare sheet filled with air and yanked her arms upwards until Belinda thought they were going to be torn off. Down and down went the hang-glider, with the wing fabric rattling uselessly over the framework of sticks.

Belinda closed her eyes and prayed as she felt herself plummeting.

Desperately she tried to pull down her arms so that she could level out the wings and get a bit of lift. Using every ounce of strength in her trained muscles, she gradually brought the wings under control. The descent slowed, and she found herself gliding, rather than falling.

The hang-glider began a slow, spiralling fall, and Belinda grew more confident. Round the tower she flew, getting lower with every circuit. The ground took on more detail. She could see trees and the outlines of fields, hedges and buildings, then clumps of flowers as she steadily sailed downward.

The princess giggled to herself. This was really quite enjoyable – what an amazing person Mulligatawny was! The warm breeze ruffled her short hair and she gazed down at the passing scene. It was all so peaceful, it was very hard to believe what was happening not so very far away.

From her position high in the sky Belinda saw the Cut-throat Robbers swarming like ants over her father's castle. She saw clouds of steam belching from the dragon – it seemed such a tiny beast from so high up – as it trundled across the drawbridge and into the palace square. A titchy figure clambered out.

That must be Bruno, thought Belinda grimly. It was time to get a move on and start a rescue bid. She put the glider into a steep dive. The wind whistled over the sheets and bits of string hummed and twanged under the strain. Belinda prayed they would hold fast.

The ground rushed closer and closer. Belinda held her breath and lowered her feet a trifle doubtfully. All at once there was a jarring shock which pushed the top half of her body straight up through the bedsheet. The wings folded over her and half a dozen bits of sticks jammed themselves between her legs. Over and over she went, with sticks snapping and sheets ripping.

Then everything ceased. Belinda lay there, hardly able to breathe inside a giant parcel of sheet, stick and string. She began to struggle until at last she squeezed her head out through a tear and gulped fresh air. She stared up at the blue sky and started to laugh. 'I've done it!' she cried. 'I've done it! No bones broken. Good old Mulligatawny!'

She quickly shuffled off the remains of the glider and made for the tower. There was no time to be lost. She must get to the top of the steps and work the lift once again. Remembering what the Robber Chief had done, she hammered on the door five times. The chains rattled and clanged. Bolts squeaked and keys grated in the ancient locks. At length the big doors were pulled back.

'Wotchawant?' demanded the old doorkeeper, glaring down at Belinda.

'Give me the horn for the lift please,' she asked politely.

The doorkeeper screwed up one eye and peered at her closely .

''Ere, I knows you, don't I? You's that princessy person. 'Ere, you're supposed to be at the top and 'ere you is at the bottom. How's you done that then?'

'Just blow the horn for the lift will you please? I'm in a hurry,' Belinda asked once more.

'Oh, oh yes, we's all in a hurry,' said the doorkeeper slowly, little realising how dangerously he was living, keeping Belinda waiting like this. 'But what I wants to know is how come you was at the top and OUCH! Urrrrff...' The doorkeeper slid slowly into a crumpled heap. Belinda had finally got fed up.

'Sorry about that,' she murmured, rubbing her hand. 'But I can't stand people who ask too many questions.'

She seized the horn and blew five times. Way

above, the lift-basket began to creak and groan on its downward journey. 'This is a much better idea than climbing all those stairs,' thought Belinda. 'Once I'm in the basket I'll be on my way. Then we'll start sorting things out. I only hope Knacker-leevee had managed to do what I whispered in his ear.'

Belinda climbed into the basket the moment it arrived and felt it jerk from the ground as it began the upward journey. It seemed an age before she could see the top of the million steps and the two enormous ape-men labouring over the winding gear.

She waited until the basket was above the platform, then leapt lightly down. There was nowhere to hide. All she could do was face up to these two bonecrushers on her own.

'Hallo!' she cried cheerfully. 'Good afternoon!'

'Eh?' The giants stopped. The lift-basket swayed gently in space as the two men turned and stared at the little princess. One of them began to grunt and snarl like a hungry hyena. The other shifted his feet and reached out toward Belinda with hands like earthmover shovels.

Belinda edged about nervously. Her feet were perilously close to the edge of the platform. One false move and either she'd be crushed by that pair of sub-human monsters, or she'd be over the lip and falling to her death at the bottom of the dark shaft.

7

This Really Is The End

Belinda grinned cheerfully at the two men. 'Hey – I heard one of you has a birthday today! Which one is it?'

'Birfday?' echoed one of the giants. 'Oo's got a birfday?'

They straightened up and began to mutter to each other with some puzzlement. Belinda seized her opportunity now that they were both off guard. 'Well, I've got presents for both of you,' she said, boldly marching straight up to them. 'Now, hold out your hands and close your eyes . . .'

The two giants shut their eyes and held out their hands. Even Belinda could hardly believe such stupidity.

'Happy Birthday!' she shouted, and WALLOP!

Before either of them could say 'Fank you, Your Highness,' they had collapsed against each other quite senseless, and were dreaming of cakes and candles.

Belinda ran to the lift handle. It was hard work, but the basket rose steadily higher and higher, until a distant shout from above told her it had reached the top. She sank panting against the unconscious giants and wiped her face, whilst she waited for

Mulligatawny, the Bogle, and the nine princesses to climb into the basket.

Getting the lift down was a lot easier. The weight of the passengers helped the descent. In fact Belinda had a hard job stopping the basket from making its own free-fall. As soon as it was safely down, Belinda raced down the spiral staircase to join everyone. Faster and faster she went, three, four, five, six steps at a time. Round and round, round and round, down to the bottom, out through the door and still she went round and round in circles, with Knackerleevee and the princesses chasing after her trying to get her to stop.

At last she fell in an exhausted, dizzy heap on the grass. The Bogle bent over her attentively. Belinda opened her eyes. The world seemed to have stopped swimming around. She sat up sharply.

'Is everyone safe? Are they all out of the tower?'

'Everyone,' cried Mulligatawny, clapping her hands. 'Oh I knew that glider would do the trick.'

Belinda turned to the Bogle. 'Did you manage to do what I suggested? Are they all ready?'

'As ready as they'll ever be,' grunted Knackerleevee with an enormous grin. 'Won't Saramanda be surprised! Biff and baff we'll go!' He smote the air with his hairy fists.

'Come on then,' cried Belinda. 'To the rescue!'

They set off through the Deep Dark Forest, with Belinda at their head, and the nine princesses at the back. The smallest, who was only five, had to trot and run to keep up. For some strange reason the princesses all seemed to have lost their fear of Knackerleevee. In fact, before long the smallest demanded a piggy-back from him, and soon he was marching through the forest, singing loudly in his cheese-grater voice and carrying four of the princesses.

The beautiful Princess Saramanda Sneak lounged across King Stormbelly's royal couch, while his servants brought her wine and crisps. She had made them drag out the Queen's jewellery boxes too, and was sifting through them one by one. 'Oh no, I don't like that bracelet at all – sapphires, how vulgar. Ah, what's this – diamonds? Yes! DIAMONDS! I adore diamonds!' Saramanda held up the ear-rings and drooled over them.

Bruno de Bruno was doing press-ups in the corner, he'd got up to forty-two, and generally flexing his muscles. It was quite true to say that he was a devastatingly handsome prince. Shame about the brain.

At this point there was a loud disturbance outside the palace and a series of soft thuds as if someone was kicking a football against a wall. There seemed to be a lot of shouting and yelling too, Saramanda got to her feet and looked out of the window. The colour drained from her face in an instant.

'I don't believe it! It's that pimple-faced Belinda, and she's got Mulligatawny and the princesses with her! Guards! Guards! To the courtyard!' Unfortunately for Saramanda the guards were already in the courtyard, though most of them were hospital-cases already. That was what all the soft thudding was about – it was the guards being thrown against the wall.

When no guards appeared Saramanda went purple. 'Bruno, get into that dragon double quick! Come on you lousy robbers, it's time to cut a few throats!' She raced off, while the Cut-throat Robbers spilled out of every room, poured down the stairs and out into the courtyard. A merry old scene was taking place there.

Belinda, Knackerleevee, the old lady and the nine princesses were standing in a small circle, with their backs to each other, while Saramanda's troops came at them from every direction. The Bogle had done exactly as Belinda had asked, and given Mulligatawny and the princesses a lightning lesson in Instant Karate for Beginners; Parts One, Two and Three.

It was just too awful to watch. Bodies flew every whichway. Stretcher-bearers raced backwards and forwards doing double overtime. Robbers staggered about clasping bruised arms and sporting magnificent black eyes. The Cut-throat band was slowly reduced to a large pile of unconscious and semi-conscious men, which looked more like a huge heap of soggy porridge than anything like fierce robbers.

The last robber collapsed on his knees and begged for mercy. Silence drifted down over the scene. Someone began to clap. It was Saramanda, standing on the balcony and watching.

'I suppose you think you're clever, Belinda

dear,' she crooned. 'It's such a shame your brain is as second-rate as your looks. It's all very well to go chip-chopping all over the place, but what are you going to do about *this*?'

Down below, doors were flung open. A huge burst of flame leapt towards Belinda and her followers. Steam hissed out and the great dragon lurched forward. The nine princesses ran shrieking from the spot and took cover. Saramanda threw back her head and laughed.

'Give yourselves up before you get yourselves fried like sausages!'

Belinda took a step back, thinking hard. Even Knackerleevee looked a trifle scared for once.

'What do we do now, Royalness?'

But Belinda was silent. It was the little old lady who had the answer.

'See where all the steam is coming from? That's the funnel for the boiler. Bruno has to let out the steam or there'll be too much pressure and the boiler will explode. Ooops!' She leapt in the air as a tongue of flame shot beneath her feet.

The Karate Princess grinned and nodded. 'I get the idea. Okay, Knackerleevee, we'll split up. Try and stay in front of the dragon. Keep Bruno's attention – oh, and Knackerleevee?'

'Yes Lindaness?'

'Don't get yourself frazzled.'

The big Bogle showed all his black teeth in a

grin and began to dance about in front of the dragon. Belinda carefully studied the metal monster until she had located the boiler funnel. When she was certain she knew what she was aiming for she gathered up what was left of the Cut-throat Robbers' hats. 'At last these can be put to good use,' she said smiling to herself.

'Bruno!' yelled Saramanda from the balcony. 'Watch out for that devil Belinda – she's up to something. Round this way, no, not that way you oaf, get the snout round this way. Go on, frazzle her up! Give her a sizzle, go on, quick!'

But it was already too late. Belinda dashed forward and threw herself upon the dragon, clawing her way up the hot metal sides. Then she was on the top and working towards the boiler funnel. The cockpit was suddenly flung back and Bruno de Bruno poked out his ridiculously handsome head. 'I say, you can't Ooooff f!' The prince went cross-eyed and sank into a deep sleep, helped along no doubt by the blow Belinda had just given him.

'I've always wanted to do that!' she laughed, edging forward once more. She seized a fistful of hats and rammed them down the funnel. A gurgling noise began to boil up inside the dragon. Belinda pushed down hat after hat until the whole beast was rumbling and grunting and shuddering with the most immense indigestion.

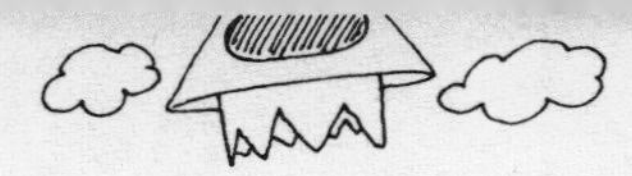

Belinda leapt lightly down and ran to Knacker-leevee and the old lady. 'Put your fingers in your ears,' warned Mulligatawny.

'What?' asked the Bogle, who had just put his fingers in his ears. 'What did you say?'

Bits of dragon were blown sky-high. A flurry of enormous hats rained down upon the courtyard. Bruno de Bruno Bunkum Krust shot into the air like a rocket, turned a neat somersault and gracefully landed in Saramanda's lap, knocking her quite senseless. Little pieces of dragon rained down for several seconds. Then there was peace.

Knackerleevee tugged at Mulligatawny's arm. 'What did you say?' he asked again.

But he never got an answer. They were suddenly swamped by the nine princesses, kissing and hugging them and demanding autographs. Bruno de Bruno gazed, with a soot-smeared face, at the cheering crowd and decided to escape while he had the chance. He grabbed Saramanda's feet and, dragging her behind, he crawled away through the castle gate. It was a very unceremonious way for a high-born princess to travel, but a few minutes later Bruno picked her up, threw her over his shoulder and disappeared, limping, into the deep dark forest.

Out from the palace came King Stormbelly, the Queen and Hubert. They had obviously had quite enough of the broom cupboard. Hubert was still wearing the mop-bucket on one foot.

'Huh, you took your time, didn't you?' rasped the King. Belinda laughed and kissed him on the forehead, which he immediately tried to rub off, while Knackerleevee suddenly growled and dashed off.

'Where's he gone?' asked the Queen.

But a moment later the Bogle reappeared, with the Queen's birthday cake, covered with glittering candles, triumphantly held aloft. His face had a ridiculous grin and he was singing *Happy Birthday* at the top of his voice. Most people put their fingers in their ears and politely waited until he had stopped. 'Who's for a slice of cake?' he asked at the end.

Knackerleevee carefully placed the cake in the middle of a table and raised one hairy arm into the air. Belinda gave a squeal.

'No Knackerleevee, use a . . .'

SPLAFF!!

Birthday cake went everywhere as the Bogle tried to slice it with a quick karate chop to the centre. Cake stuck to the ceiling, slid down the walls, and plastered everyone in the hall with bits of sponge and icing.

'... a knife,' murmured Belinda, licking some jam-filling from the tip of her nose.

King Stormbelly took a long-suffering look at everyone and they waited for him to fly into one of his famous temper-tantrums. But he burst out laughing and once started he couldn't stop. When the Queen tucked him up in bed that night he was still giggling. He only stopped when he saw his sixteenth daughter.

'So when *are* you going to get married then?' he demanded.

'Oh Dad,' groaned the Karate Princess. 'Go to sleep!'

Also in Puffin

A RAT'S TALE

Tor Seidler

Montague Mad-Rat lives in a sewer in New York City, where his family are improverished but creative. His life is very sheltered until he meets Isabel Moberly Rat who changes all this. Isabel is a wharf rat, enjoying a much richer lifestyle, but Montague realizes that her home will soon be turned into a car park and, because of his love for her, plans to act immediately. But he is hindered by his background, so how can he possibly save Isabel and Ratdom, and win her love at the same time?

THE GOLDEN JOURNEY

John Rowe Townsend

Eleni has always been different from all the other people on her island but she never dreamt that she would be chosen by the gods to be the messenger to save her island from a war that is destroying them.

DODOS ARE FOREVER

Dick King-Smith

Once upon a time (about 300 years ago) Dodos lived happily on an island in the Indian Ocean. Then one day Man arrived (and more importantly, rats arrived too) and the happy, peaceful life of the Dodos would never be the same again. This is the riveting, funny, tragic tale of the demise of the Dodos – and of one small group of birds that (according to Dick King-Smith) made their escape and set up a new colony on a nearby island.

DOWNHILL ALL THE WAY

K. M. Peyton

The chance of a school skiing trip to France means different things to different people. Nutty and David can't wait to go. Jean isn't sure about it, and Hoomey is not keen at all. But eventually they do arrive in the ski resort of Claribel, and their experiences as first-time skiers make hilarious reading.

SNAPS KELLY AND THE PAPER MONSTERS

Joseph Ducke

Snaps Kelly lives with his decidedly eccentric grandpa in an equally eccentric house in London. Snaps is a fairly ordinary boy, until one hot summer the paper monsters arrive! Suddenly he has to become an ace detective, determined to discover why all the paper in London is dissolving. With no newspapers, no underground tickets, no toilet paper(!) and worse still, no money, daily life is changing dramatically. Meanwhile, the evil Dr Chengappa is always one step ahead and it looks as though life in the civilized world could be changed forever.

A PACK OF LIARS

Anne Fine

When Laura's teacher sets up a pen pal scheme, Laura finds herself in correspondence with an extremely boring girl called Miranda. Desperate, Laura decides to liven things up by pretending to be a Lady Melody from a noble and wealthy family. Her friend, Oliver, is horrified at her pack of lies and makes her feel so guilty that she tries to make amends by visiting her pen pal personally, only to discover that Miranda is a professional thief who steals from the rich to give to the poor! The plan to expose her makes entertaining and gripping reading.